This Little Tiger book
belongs to:

_____

_____

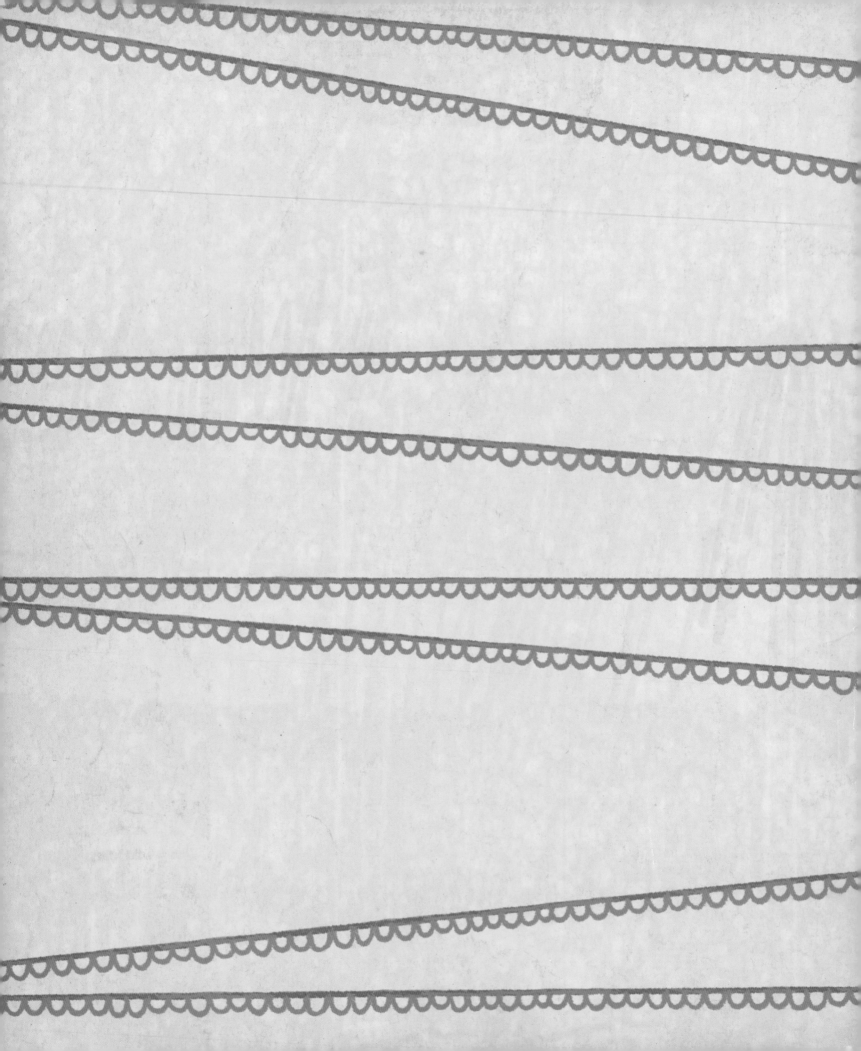

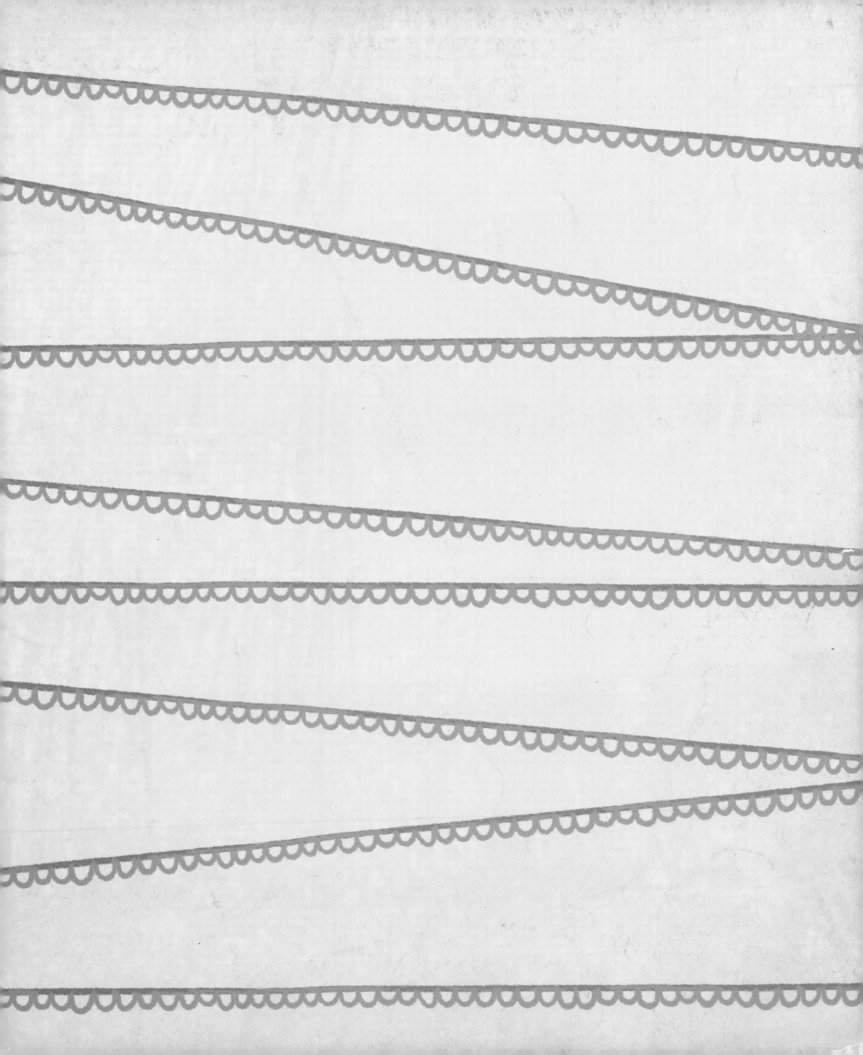

For Avery and Henry, who are both cock-a-doo-delightful! - S S

To my smart family and friends who understand that
drawing animals and poop is the best job ever - F W

LITTLE TIGER PRESS LTD,
an imprint of the Little Tiger Group
1 Coda Studios
189 Munster Road
London SW6 6AW
www.littletiger.co.uk

First published in Great Britain 2018
This edition published 2018
Text copyright © Steve Smallman 2018
Illustrations copyright © Florence Weiser 2018
Steve Smallman and Florence Weiser have asserted their rights
to be identified as the author and illustrator of this work
under the Copyright, Designs and Patents Act, 1988
A CIP catalogue record for this book
is available from the British Library

ISBN 978-1-84869-828-4
LTP/1400/2180/0418
Printed in China
10 9 8 7 6 5 4 3 2 1

# CoCk-a-dOoDle-Poo!

Steve Smallman

Florence Weiser

LiTTLE TiGER

LONDON

**Down** on the farm there's a **terrible** pong.
(Well, the animals are pooing there all day long!)

**Splat!**

What's that?

It's a **big**
cow pat,

And
the sheep
pop
pellets
out –
rat-a-tat-a-tat!

Pig keeps **plopping** like he's never ever stopping,
And you'd better stand clear
when a horse poo's **dropping!**

Farmer Jill says,
"What you have to understand
Is it might **pong** a bit
but it's **good for the land!**"

But it wasn't so good for
the chickens on the ground,

Dodging bits of **doo-doo** flying **all around!**

"Oh, I wish I could fly where the air is clear," groaned Rooster.

"The pong's too strong down here!"

One day, Jill came back from the city
With a new hair cut – she looked so **pretty!**

Then somebody cried out,

"CoCk-a- dOoDle-

doo- dOO!"

And **plopped** on the top
of her nice
new **hairdo!**

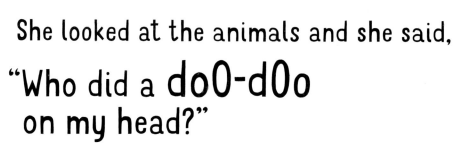

She looked at the animals and she said,
"Who did a doO-dOo
on my head?"

Horse said, "I heard
'CoCk-a-dOoDle-
doo-dOO!'"

"Rooster!" Sheep cried.
"That's what **you** do!"

"Well, it can't be **him**!"
said Hen with a smirk,
"Everybody knows that
his wings don't work.

"Chickens can run,
and flap, and JUMP!

But we can't fly high because
we're just too
plump!"

Jill shampooed
the POO from her hair,

And cried,
"What's happened
to my UNDERWEAR?

I left my knickers on the line to dry,
So where did they go to?
Pants can't fly!"

Rooster was hiding,
he felt really bad,
He hadn't meant to doo-doo
on the farmer but he had.

First he'd pinched her **knickers**
and he'd pulled out **the elastic,**

To make a **rooster**
**booster**
**catapult**
(it was fantastic!).

It shot

him up into the sky,

he flew a loOp-the-loOp,

He cried out, "CoCk-a-dOoDle-dOo!"

and then he did a poop!

"From now on," he decided,
"I will only fly at night,
In case I have another little
accident in flight!"

So he waited till the **moon** came out
but by its light he saw,
A hungry fox was sneaking

to the
creaking
hen house
door!

Rooster put his goggles on
and shouted, "Time to fly!"

He catapulted off the roof and up into the sky.

"I'll save you, hens!" he cried,
and Fox laughed,
"Really? What can you do?"

"Funny you should ask,"
said Rooster.

"CoCk-a-
dOoDle-dOo-
doO!"

Everyone was woken by the sound
of Rooster CROWING!
So much poop was falling that
they thought it must be snowing!

The poor old fox was **flattened** by the massive

PoOp atTACk.

He ran away and Rooster cried, "Clear off and don't come back!"

"You've saved the day!" cheered Farmer Jill.
    "But I don't understand,
However did you fly so high?
However will you land?"

        But Rooster wasn't worried.
            No, he couldn't give a hoot.

    The farmer's
        frilly knickers
            made . . .

...a perfect **parachute!**

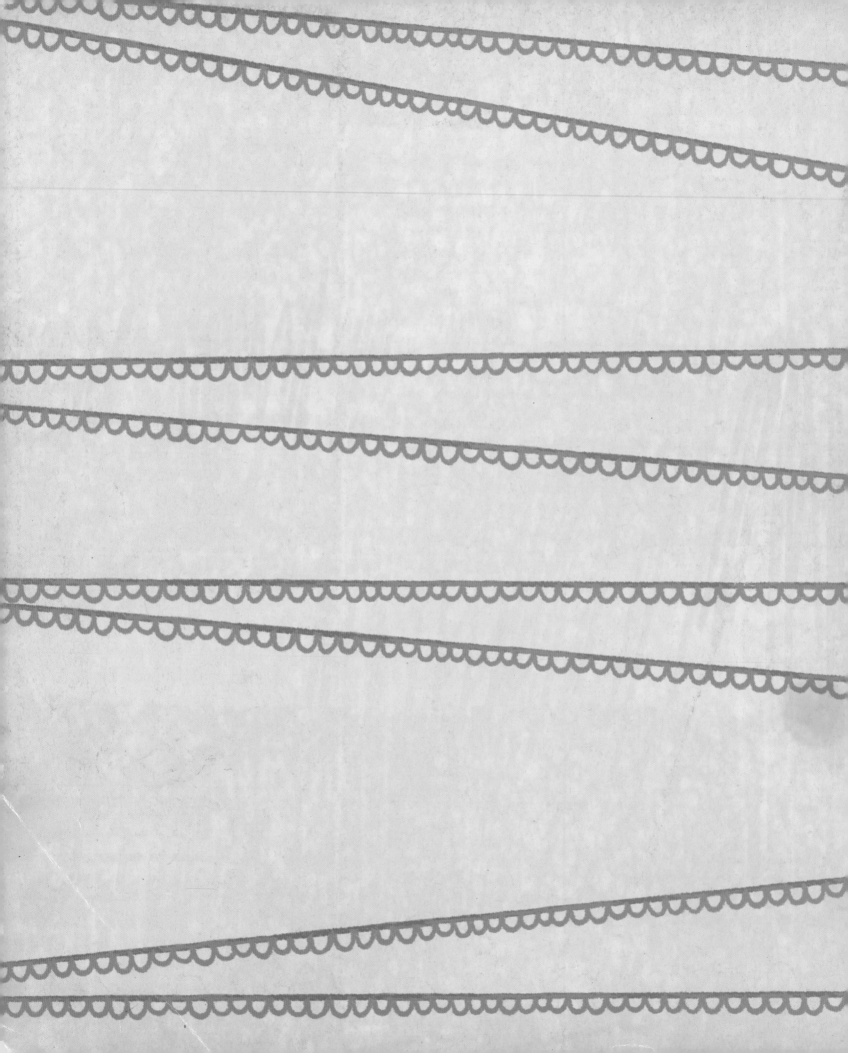

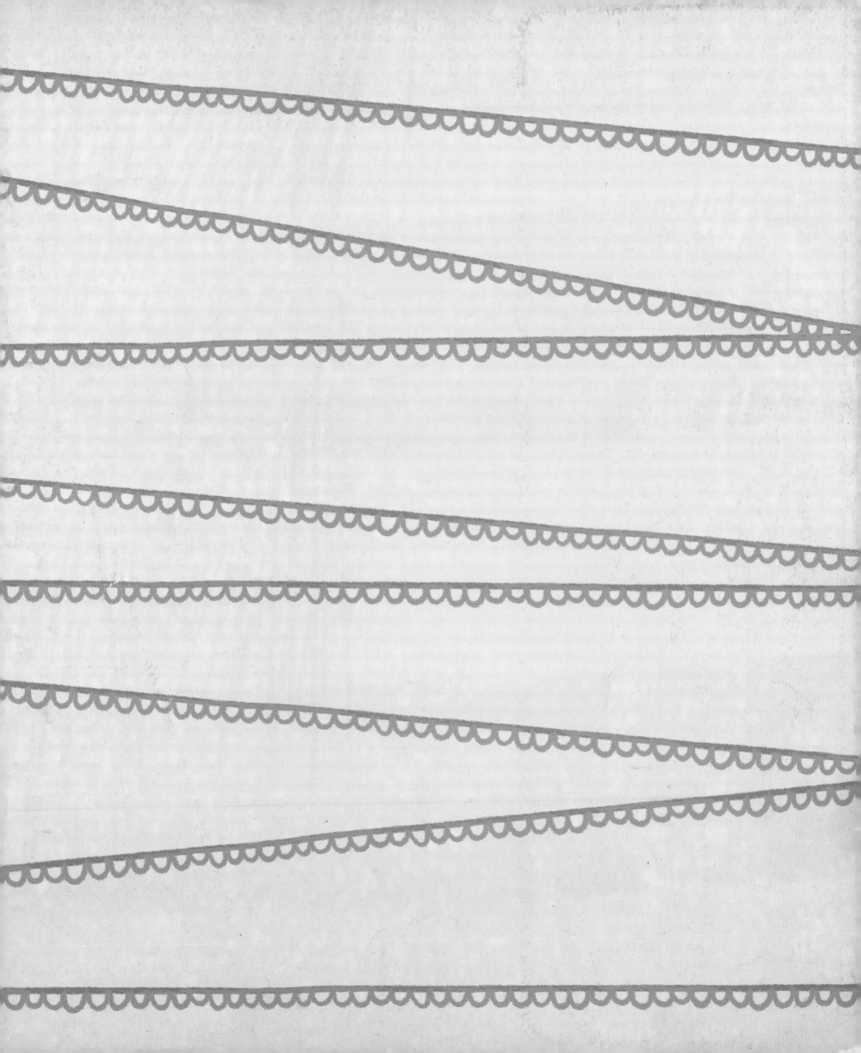

# More fun and frolics from Little Tiger Press!

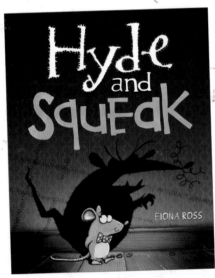

For information regarding any of the above titles or for our catalogue, please contact us:
Little Tiger Press, 1 Coda Studios, 189 Munster Road, London SW6 6AW
Tel: 020 7385 6333 • E-mail: contact@littletiger.co.uk • www.littletiger.co.uk